ROBIN HOOD
AND HIS MERRIE MEN

Retold by
ROGER DUNLOP

Illustrated by
JOHN LEEDER

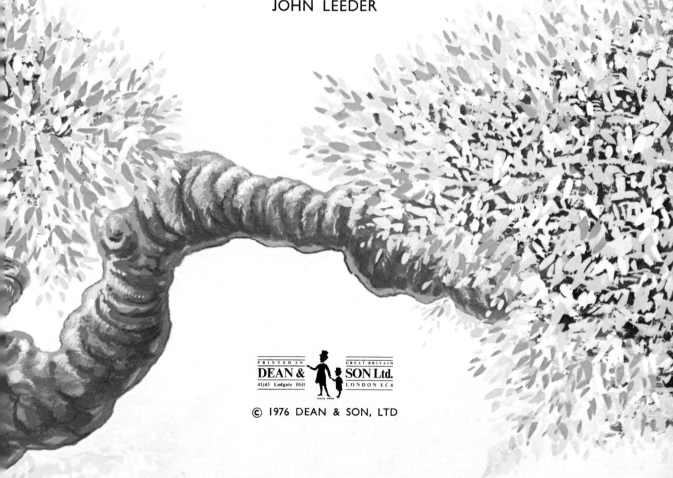

PRINTED IN GREAT BRITAIN
DEAN & SON Ltd.
41/43 Ludgate Hill   LONDON EC4
TRADE MARK

© 1976 DEAN & SON, LTD

ONE day, when Robin Hood was a boy, his mother told him how her uncle, Sir Guy of Coventry, had gone into the forest to attack, single-handed, a wild blue boar that had killed several people. Alone, he had trapped the beast and, after plunging a long knife into its heart, he'd carried home its grizzly head, with its enormous tusks, as a trophy.

Young Robin, impressed by his ancestor's bravery, went, then and there, into Sherwood Forest. He was away so long that his parents began to worry about him, and his father was just setting out to search for him when he came home. "Where have you been?" thundered his father.

"I went deep into the forest to see if I could find and slay a wild boar as Sir Guy did."

"It was brave of you to seek the boar, but lucky for you and for us who love you that you didn't meet him," said his father more gently.

"I met some rough men in the forest who gave me food and drink," said Robin, "and they said that perhaps one day I'd live in the forest myself."

"Heaven forbid!" cried his mother.

Through the years, while he was growing into sturdy manhood, Robin never forgot that first adventure in the forest. He spent his leisure time wrestling, leaping, running, fighting with sticks and big poles, and became an expert horseman. But his favourite sport was with his bow-and-arrows, aiming at a target.

When Robin was old enough to protect his mother from bands of robbers on the road, his father agreed to let him escort her on a visit to her brother, Squire Gamwell, of Gamwell Hall, near Nottingham. Squire Gamwell was a good man, fond of youngsters, and Robin's mother wanted to show her sturdy son to him. The horse was prepared, loaded with food and drink to last them the forty-mile journey, then Robin, his dagger in his belt and wearing a sword his father had given him, sprang into the saddle while his mother was lifted onto the pillion behind him, and off they went, and in due course they reached Gamwell Hall safely.

Robin's uncle was delighted to see his sister and his nephew, and introduced Robin to his son, Will, a tall, fair-haired youth, and the two cousins became firm friends.

Next day, Will's cousin, Maid Marian, came to stay at Gamwell Hall for a week. Robin liked her at once; she was not only pretty and lady-like, she also enjoyed boys' games and was a good markswoman with the bow-and-arrow. Many people were invited to a feast at Gamwell Hall, and Maid Marian, who was the most beautiful girl present, was made Queen of Ceremonies. She commanded the young men to match their strength against one another, and when Robin won every contest, including quarter-staff fighting and sword-play, she cried "Bravo!" And her only remaining wish was that he should win the archery contest. Robin promptly hit the bull's-eye, but so did the arrows of some other fellows. To determine the winner, Robin made a suggestion to Marian, who thought it was such a good idea she said, "I command that a slender willow-rod be placed in the ground, and whoever hits it with his arrow from forty paces shall be the winner!"

The other young men thought it couldn't be done, but Robin, drawing his bow and taking aim, split the willow-rod in two with his arrow! There was loud applause, and Robin's mother and Maid Marian were both very proud of his skill.

While Robin and his mother were staying at Gamwell Hall, he and Marian heard that a fair was being held in Nottingham. "We must go," said Robin. "You'll get a poor welcome from the townspeople," warned Will Gamwell. "Every year we go to the fair, but the stupid Nottingham people look down on people from the villages, like us, and there's usually trouble."

When the fair was in full swing, a party of youths, headed by Robin and Marian, walked into Nottingham, and groups of youths from the town started to hurl insults at Robin and his friends. Robin, who had never seen a fair before, ignored the insults for a while, but when other townsfolk began to jeer at them, Robin and his friends were infuriated and turned over three of the stalls. Immediately, the townsfolk, armed with staves, attacked Robin's band, and in the fighting that followed a man was killed. "Robin! Come away!" yelled his friends. But Robin was too busy fighting to heed.

Presently, the Sheriff came on the scene, arrested Robin, told him he'd be charged with killing the man, and ordered his men to throw him in prison.

As he sat in his cell, Robin's first thought was to wonder if Marian had escaped. Then, thinking of making his own escape, he looked about him. Like all prisons in his time, this one was made of timber and the roof was full of holes. So when it was dark he climbed through the straw-thatched roof, slid to the ground, ran back to his uncle's house, said farewell to Marian, placed his mother on his horse and rode home. But not wanting to bring his father into conflict with the Sheriff, he hid in the forest—and thus began his exciting adventures as an outlaw.

"Take him, dead or alive!" ordered the Sheriff, when he heard of Robin's escape, and his men set off in pursuit. When they came to the cottage where

Robin lived, they were met by Robin's father.

"We have orders to arrest Robin Hood," said the leader. "We demand, in the name of His Majesty the King, that you hand him over to us."

"He's not here," replied Robin's father. "He's in the forest. If you venture there, take care, for hidden marksmen might be lurking behind every tree." In spite of any wrong Robin had done, his father was trying to protect him by dissuading the Sheriff's men from going into the forest. And indeed, when they came to the edge of the forest, they decided it would be safer to return to Nottingham.

Robin had entered the forest in the evening, let a spark from his flint and steel fall on a piece of tinder-wood he kept in his box, placed the smouldering tinder in some dry leaves and brushwood and soon had a bright fire, the glow from which attracted some other outlaws. When they approached, Robin told them he was a fugitive from the Sheriff of Nottingham. "We live on the King's deer, and the venison from it," said the men, inviting him to eat with them.

Robin joined the outlaws and became their captain, and the story of his escape into the forest spread far and wide, and soon many villagers, oppressed by the harsh feudal laws, joined Robin, who made sure they had only the finest arrows and the best bows made of pliable yew. He also made them proficient with their weapons, which, besides arrows, included short swords. Then he said they'd be less likely to be noticed if they all wore green, as that would blend with the grass and leaves of the forest.

Robin was a born leader, which wasn't surprising, for his father was related to a noble family, and but for twists of fortune in relation to his mother's ancestors—the death of someone here, the marriage of someone there—he'd have become the Earl of Huntingdon.

Later, Robin showed his men how, by blowing his horn in different ways, messages could be sent. Sharp blasts meant a cry for help; two notes sounded in quick succession meant someone was calling; three sharp blasts meant Robin wanted to speak to his men.

When the outlaws numbered a hundred and forty, Robin said that outside the forest there were many bad men, bad things, bad ways. "Let us go and alter them! Let us right the wrongs done to the poor," he cried, and they pledged their word to support him.

In his new suit of Lincoln green, Robin told Much-the-Miller's son, one of his band, that he was going out-side the forest, and reminded his men to listen for his horn, should there be trouble. He followed a stream and started to cross a wooden bridge. But then he stopped, for starting to cross at the opposite end was a giant of a man. "Let me pass, fellow!" com-manded Robin, glancing at the stream below.

The giant didn't move, then, as Robin fitted an arrow to his bow, the big man lumbered towards him, a quarter-staff in his hands. "If you dare to shoot the arrow," he said, "I'll dust the hide off you."

They were brave words, for Robin, with his bow, had the advantage. Robin admired his courage. "You are a coward," said the giant. "You are armed with bow-and-arrows, while I have only my staff."

"Coward!" laughed Robin. "I'll show you I'm no coward."

Robin leapt off the bridge, sprang at a branch of a tree, and by sheer strength tore it down, and the two rained blows at each other. Then Robin missed his footing and fell into the stream. "You proved your-self the better man this time," said Robin.

The giant, whose name was John Little, was out

of work and hungry. "Come back with me," said Robin, "and you'll have a good meal."

As they reached Sherwood Forest, Robin blew three blasts on his horn; other horns answered his call, and soon a crowd of men dressed like himself surrounded them. "Meet my merry men, John Little," said Robin. "Come, join us; there's plenty to eat and drink, and as for work—well, we fight tyrants and those who rob the poor."

John Little was keen to join, and Robin said they must re-christen him, and at Will-the-Wrestler's suggestion they called him Little John. They dressed him in a suit of Lincoln green, taught him to shoot, and how to use his sword and dagger, and he soon became a great favourite with the outlaws. Robin often left him in command while he went off by himself. The men respected the giant, whose strength was enormous, and they were satisfied

to have one so brave and strong as their leader when Robin was away.

Little John never again knew what it was to be hungry, for Robin Hood and his merry outlaws dined richly off the King's deer, which they shot in their forest home.

Passing one day through Sherwood Forest, a traveller was ambushed and captured by Robin Hood's men. Little John tied his hands tightly behind him and marched him through the forest with his bundles and horse. Robin was angry when he examined the traveller. "Who tied this man's hands behind him in this ruthless manner?" he demanded, and when Little John admitted that *he'd* done it, Robin ordered his men to seize the giant and tie his hands behind his back, as he had tied those of the traveller. His bonds cut deeply into his wrists. Then Robin said, "Now, Little John, how do you like it, yourself? Was it necessary to tie the captive's hands so tightly? In future, never handle

people too roughly. While I want strong men, they must always have gentle hearts. You've had your lesson and now you'll be freed. And remember—*all* of you—never be rough with prisoners."

When Little John was freed, he apologized to the traveller, whose bonds were cut, too. In answer to a question from Robin, the traveller said, "I left Nottingham this morning with bundles of coarse cloth to sell to the labourers and their women in the villages."

"Then you were not going to sell fine and dainty clothes to the squires of the district and their ladies?" queried Robin.

"Certainly not," said the man. "Had I done so, they might have taken what they wanted and refused to pay me."

Robin nodded. "Open his pack," he said to the men, "and if he's spoken the truth, I'll set him free, for we have no wish to wage war on the poor."

The man had spoken the truth, for when the pack was opened it contained only bales of russet-browns, cloth of grey and drab, such as common folk would wear. As he rode away the merchant promised to bring some bales of Lincoln green, and, keeping his word, he returned with the cloth, and the outlaws paid him in full for the material.

A few days later he was back, complaining that he'd been set upon by a band of robbers who'd taken his money and his horse. But when the merchant took Robin and his men to the spot where he said he'd been ambushed, they found no signs of a struggle, and Robin, becoming suspicious, sent two of his men to visit the merchant's house in town.

"The man's lied," said the men when they returned. "His horse is in his stable."

"You lied, hoping to get money out of us," said Robin, "and you'll stay here until someone from your home brings the profit you made on the cloth you sold to us. We only want the profit—we wouldn't dream of robbing you of what the cloth cost to begin with."

Robin's terms were carried out, and the merchant was released. By this example, Robin's men realized that it wasn't his intention to hurt ploughman or labourer, or even a high-born knight, providing he was honest and good. "Help good folk, and those who find life difficult," said Robin to his band, "but treat those who make it difficult as our enemies—with the Sheriff of Nottingham as the chief!"

A tall but shabby knight, called Sir Richard of Lea, rode into Sherwood Forest on a fine black horse. Soon he was waylaid by Little John, who took him to Robin. Knights were sometimes rich and cruel, and the outlaws often took their wealth from them to give to the poor. But Sir Richard was neither rich nor cruel.

Robin gave him a meal and asked him how much money he had. "Ten shillings," replied Sir Richard—and when his bags were searched that was indeed all he did possess. Then Sir Richard told Robin his story. "I was once a rich man," he said, "but many of my cattle died, much of my wealth was stolen, and my son, who accidentally killed a knight in a tournament, was threatened with prison unless he could pay a heavy fine. To save him from prison, I had to borrow the money from an Abbot, but I had to promise to pay it back before a certain day or I'd have to hand over to him all my lands. That day is to-morrow, and as I can't pay, I'm going to the Abbot—whose abbey is near Nottingham—to hand over all my lands. I owe him four hundred pounds."

"I believe your story, and I'll lend you the money, for I know you'll repay me when you can," said Robin. Turning to Little John, he said, "Bring me four hundred pounds out of our treasure-chest and place it in a bag."

The knight, who was overcome with gratitude, was a happy man as he rode away through the greenwood that day.

"To-day's the day!" sang the Abbot the next morning. "By twelve o'clock, I'll be a very rich man with lands here, there, and everywhere!" The cunning Abbot had learned that the knight was in no position to pay; besides, the lands that would fall into his hands would be far more useful to him than the money. He was sure that the knight wouldn't be able to pay, and had the magistrate with him so that he could witness the handing-over of Sir Richard's lands. But then, as it neared twelve o'clock, Sir Richard arrived and surprised the greedy Abbot by paying the debt in full, and the magistrate ordered the Abbot to give Sir Richard the deed he'd signed.

As Sir Richard had come through Sherwood Forest without being robbed by Robin Hood, the Abbot thought it would be safe for him to take his money through the forest and trade it at a profit in Nottingham. So, distributing his wealth among forty-nine of his armed men (while he himself carried only twenty coins), they all set off. But they were ambushed by the outlaws and taken to Robin's camp. Robin gave the Abbot and his men a sumptuous feast, and when they'd eaten he said, "My guests always pay something towards the meals they have with us. If they're poor, they pay nothing, but rich men pay heavily both for their own meals and for those before them who had theirs free."

The Abbot swore he had very little money, but when the outlaws searched the packs of the Abbot's men, Robin knew he was lying, so he charged him five pounds a head for the meal, plus a fine of a hundred and fifty pounds for not telling the truth. "Strangely, the total sum is the same that Sir Richard paid to you as a debt!" said Robin.

The Abbot paid the price and departed.

When Sir Richard retrieved his fortunes, he went to repay Robin, but Robin told him the debt had been paid by the Abbot while on his way to Nottingham!

Robin longed to see Maid Marian again. He knew she was staying at Gamwell Hall as Squire Gamwell's guest, her father having been killed while helping to defend Gamwell Hall in a battle between the Sheriff's men and Squire Gamwell's men. So Robin and Little John set off, and were warmly welcomed by the Squire, Will Gamwell, and Marian. While Robin and Little John were there the Sheriff's men surrounded Gamwell Hall. That night, when it was dark, Robin, Little John, and some of the Squire's men swam the moat, attacked the Sheriff's men, and returned to the Hall. But one of the Squire's men had been captured by the Sheriff's men, so next morning, as the captive was about to be hanged, Robin and Will, with their arrows, killed the men guarding him, and he made good his escape back to the Hall.

The Sheriff was furious and vowed he'd take Robin Hood with his own hands. "If the Sheriff wants to see me," said Robin, "I'll make certain that he does!"

Marian, who loved Robin, begged him to do nothing rash. But Robin had made his mind up, and, leaving Little John to look after the girl, he left Gamwell Hall. On his way, he paid a handsome price to a butcher for his horse and cart loaded with meat. He also bought the butcher's ragged clothes, giving him his own in exchange.

Disguised in the butcher's clothes, Robin drove the horse and cart into Nottingham, and, setting up his stall beside the other butchers, he shouted, "Prime beef for sale! Lovely loins of lamb! A penny a pig!" Crowds flocked round his stall to buy his cheap meat, but the other butchers were furious, declaring he was spoiling their trade.

"I'm a poor farmer and thought I'd sell my meat cheap to make some extra profit," said Robin, when the Sheriff came to see what all the commotion was about.

The Sheriff, who thought this butcher must be stupid to think he'd make a profit by selling his meat at such low prices, asked Robin how many cattle he had. "Well over a hundred," said Robin.

"Why not sell me your beasts?" said the Sheriff, thinking *he'd* make some money out of this simpleton of a butcher.

Robin said he'd sell his beasts for three hundred pounds, and agreed to show them to the Sheriff. When they reached Sherwood Forest, Robin blew three blasts on his horn and, pointing to the King's deer, said, "That's my herd of beasts!" When they were surrounded by the outlaws he said, "You've wanted to meet Robin Hood—well, here I am!"

They blindfolded the Sheriff, took him to the outlaws' camp, gave him a meal off the King's deer—which didn't seem to trouble him—then Robin asked him to pay for the beasts.

"You tricked me," said the Sheriff. "We were talking of cattle."

"*I* never mentioned cattle," said Robin. "I referred to beasts, and beasts they are."

Robin's men took the three hundred pounds off the Sheriff, then, blindfolding him again, led him out of the forest and set him free. "I'll catch Robin Hood if it's the last thing I do!" vowed the Sheriff, as he entered Nottingham.

One day, while Robin was on the edge of the forest, he stood and watched while a young man in silk doublet and scarlet stockings killed one of the King's deer with an arrow. "Well hit!" cried Robin.

The young man spun round and threatened Robin with an arrow through the ribs if he didn't clear off. But when Robin didn't move, the man in scarlet challenged him to a fight. "Unsheath your blade then, and I'll cross swords with you," said Robin.

As their blades clashed, Robin realized that his opponent was a fine swordsman, and thought he was just the man for his band. The fight ended when, with one terrific stroke, Robin crashed the other man's sword to the ground. Then, dropping his own weapon (for he had no wish to harm him), he said, "A life of adventure would suit you."

"That's why I'm here," exclaimed the other. "I came to join Robin Hood's band. You see, I left home because, by accident, I nearly killed one of my father's servants. If he lives, all will be well; but if he dies, I'll dangle at the end of a rope."

"That's a good enough reason for wanting to join my band," said Robin.

The other was nonplussed. "Then *you're* Robin Hood!"

"Come, and I'll introduce you to my men," smiled Robin.

The youth, whose Christian name was William, was welcomed by the outlaws, and after they'd given him a meal Robin, looking at his stockings, re-christened him Will Scarlet.

On one occasion, while Robin was sitting by the side of a forest stream, he heard two men arguing. "One of the best streams in the country," said one voice.

"Ridiculous!" said the other. "There's not a fish in the whole stream."

The voices came nearer, and a very fat friar with an almost bald head came into view. He was alone; there was no sign of a second man. "It's useless to fish in this stream," said the friar. Then, answering himself, he said, "Take me to a better one!" He was arguing with himself!

"Good morning," called Robin. "How are you both?"

"Oh, we're fine," returned the friar.

Robin ordered the friar to carry him across the stream. When they reached the other side, the friar, brandishing his sword, said, "Now it's my turn. I want to cross the stream, and you're going to carry me."

Robin slid into the water and struggled

across the stream with the fat friar on his back. "Now," said Robin, "you're going to carry me back again across the stream."

"For the last time!" declared the friar.

Robin clambered on the fat man's back, but the friar's step wasn't quite so steady this time, and just over halfway across he tripped on a stone, fell forward, and Robin was pitched clean off his broad back, and fell with a splash in the water, while the holy man waded towards the bank and climbed out.

After a short fist fight started by Robin because he thought the friar had tossed him in the water on purpose, they shook hands and became friends, then Robin blew three blasts on his horn, and Little John was the first to arrive on the scene. "Why, it's my old friend, Friar Tuck, one of the best archers!" exclaimed Little John.

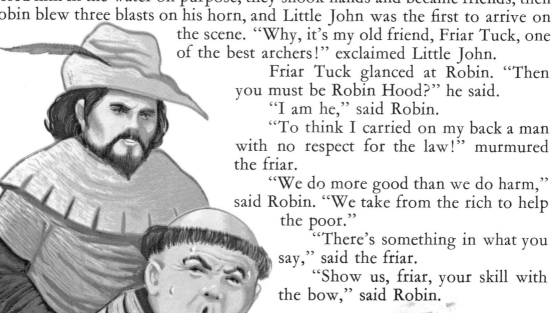

Friar Tuck glanced at Robin. "Then you must be Robin Hood?" he said.

"I am he," said Robin.

"To think I carried on my back a man with no respect for the law!" murmured the friar.

"We do more good than we do harm," said Robin. "We take from the rich to help the poor."

"There's something in what you say," said the friar.

"Show us, friar, your skill with the bow," said Robin.

Friar Tuck whistled and his dog bounded towards him and stood perfectly still with a stone on its head, then the friar fired an arrow, knocking the stone off the animal's head. The dog was untouched.

"A perfect shot!" said Robin. "Will you join my band? We need a chaplain to help us to mend some of our wicked ways."

"I'll join you, if you think I'll be useful," said Friar Tuck—and he was almost the only member to join Robin's band without re-christening.

When an old lady Robin knew told him that Sir Guy of Gisborne had attacked Gamwell Hall, killed Squire Gamwell, and was now living there himself, and that nobody knew what had become of Maid Marian and Will Gamwell, Robin's mind was filled with revenge against the wicked knight. Refusing to believe that Maid Marian—*his* Marian—was dead, Robin mustered his men, and they set out through the forest that very night to attack Gamwell Hall.

When they reached the lighted Hall they swam the moat and waited while Little John and Will Scarlet climbed through a hole in the fence and crept up to the windows and looked inside. "Sir Guy's holding a feast," reported Little John. "They are making merry."

"They'll not be so merry when they've felt our steel," said Robin, grimly.

The outlaws tore down more of the fence until there was a hole large enough for the men to climb through in pairs. "I'm going alone to the door of

the Hall," said Robin, when all the men were standing in the grounds. "Keep silent and follow me in the shadows."

Robin went on ahead, reached the door and knocked.

"What do you want?" asked the doorkeeper, peering through the darkness at the visitor.

"Is Sir Guy at home?" asked Robin.

"He is."

"Then tell him that Robin Hood has come to see him."

"I—I'll tell Sir Guy," he stammered. "Are you alone?"

"Does it look as if anyone's with me?"

Again the doorkeeper peered into the night. He could see nobody. "Wait!" he said, and, running into the Hall, told Sir Guy.

"Tell him to come in," laughed Sir Guy. "If Robin Hood wants to put his head in a noose, let him do so!"

"I fear he has some trick up his sleeve," said the doorkeeper.

"Admit him, I say!" cried Sir Guy.

The doorkeeper said no more. He went back to the entrance and opened the door again. While he'd been talking to Sir Guy, Robin's men had crept towards their leader. Now they were all standing at the door. "Sir Guy will see you," said the doorkeeper.

"Then out of our way," cried Robin, thrusting the man aside, and the Merrie Men followed Robin down the Hall to where Sir Guy was feasting at a trestle-table with many knights. Around the walls stood a number of Sir Guy's soldiers.

Sir Guy had expected Robin to come by himself and had intended to capture him. But the sight of Robin's archers made him rise up in terror.
"Slay them!" he screamed.

"Every man for himself!" shouted Robin, rushing at the knight. A terrific fight followed. Suddenly a sword knocked an oil-lamp to the floor. Another followed, then another. Robin was grappling with Sir Guy when the last lamp fell, and in the confusion the knight escaped from the Hall. In the darkness it was impossible to follow him, for neither side could tell who was who.

Suddenly fire flared up. One of the oil-lamps had set light to the timbered walls of the Hall, and the whole building would be burning before long. "Sir Guy has escaped!" Robin shouted. "It's useless fighting on in this inferno. We must leave these rascals and return to the forest."

As the flames spread, Robin's men made their way out of the burning building, crossed the grounds and swam the moat. But two of his men were left behind, killed by Sir Guy's soldiers.

"This is a sad sight," murmured Robin to Friar Tuck, as they stood for a moment on the other side of the moat watching the flames leaping high into the air. "The Gamwell Hall that I've loved will soon be no more."

But Robin's mind wandered from the Hall. He'd set out to rescue the beautiful Maid Marian from Sir Guy of Gisborne, yet he'd seen no sign either of her or of Will Gamwell. He was a very worried man as he returned to his encampment in the forest.

The following day Sir Guy of Gisborne went back to Gamwell Hall, and when he saw that it was now a smoking ruin he rode into town to see the Sheriff of Nottingham. "I'm going to disguise myself as a traveller," said Sir Guy, "and when I meet Robin Hood I shall bring him to you alive at the point of my sword. So make the gallows ready for my return."

"How will I know you've been successful?" asked the Sheriff.

"When I've captured Robin Hood I'll blow a long note on a hunting horn," said the knight, and dressing himself in the clothes of a traveller and slinging the hunting horn round his neck, he set out alone into the forest.

That same morning Little John and Will Scarlet, disguised as poor travellers, went to Nottingham to buy some new green cloth to replace the outlaws' uniforms torn in the fight. Before they entered the town, they separated so that no suspicion would be aroused. But Will Scarlet made the mistake of buying a large quantity of the green cloth from one merchant, instead of buying small quantities of the stuff from different shops. The merchant became suspicious of this poor traveller spending so much money, and ran to the Sheriff, who ordered some of his men to chase the outlaw.

Will Scarlet, carrying his bundle, ran like the wind, with the Sheriff's men in pursuit. Suddenly, he dropped his bundle and, turning, fired two arrows in quick succession, knocking two of the men to the ground. Picking up his bundle, he ran off.

"Good shooting!" cried Little John, who was near by.

The Sheriff heard his remark and, being sure he was one of Robin's men, ordered his men to give chase, and they caught the outlaw after a fierce struggle. With his hands tied behind him, Little John was led up a hill, and the Sheriff said, "Hang him!"

In the distance, a long clear note on a horn was heard. The Sheriff was jubilant. "That horn was a signal from Sir Guy of Gisborne. It means he's captured Robin Hood. Now they'll both hang together."

Sir Guy came into view, dragging Robin along with him. "Good work, Sir Guy," cried the Sheriff.

Suddenly, Sir Guy threw off his cloak. The Sheriff stared, his eyes goggling. It wasn't Sir Guy, it was Robin Hood, and the man beside him was Will Scarlet!

Robin cut Little John free, and the three men fought their way out of the town and back

to the forest. "But, master," cried Little John, "how did you manage to put over such a daring scheme? I really thought it was the end of me—and of you."

Robin said he'd been walking along the Nottingham road when he met an old traveller who said he wasn't *really* a traveller, but Sir Guy of Gisborne and that he meant to capture Robin Hood, blow his horn to warn the Sheriff to prepare the gallows, and take him to Nottingham. Robin then revealed his identity, and after a furious fight he thrust his sword through the knight's heart, killing him.

Will Scarlet said, "When I saw that you, Little John, were about to be hanged, I ran to tell Robin, who put on Sir Guy's clothes, and we came back, as you saw, to your rescue."

All this happened the day after the burning of Gamwell Hall. Robin was still worried about Maid Marian's fate. He loved her dearly and would have asked her to marry him, but he felt it wouldn't have been right to ask Marian— a girl of gentle upbringing—to share his forest adventures. But though Robin didn't know it, Marian was in love with him, just as he was with her, and would

have followed him anywhere if he'd asked her. But she thought he preferred to live a wild life with his men in the forest.

When Sir Guy of Gisborne attacked Gamwell Hall, Maid Marian and Will Gamwell had been away visiting relatives. When they returned to find the Hall burned down and Squire Gamwell killed, they realized that they were now without a home. Will Gamwell said he'd avenge his father's death by joining Robin Hood in the forest, and Maid Marian, who'd lost her parents, her home, everything, said she was going with him.

Packing their few belongings, they entered the forest that afternoon, and came to Robin Hood's camp in the early evening.

"We have visitors, master!" cried Much-the-Miller's son, as he saw the two figures approaching.

Robin came into the glade. "Marian!" His face broke into a happy smile as he ran to meet the girl.

After Marian and Will had told Robin all they'd done since they last saw him, they told him of their decision to join the Merrie Men. Robin was delighted. "Let me show you how we live," he said. He took them round the camp, introduced them to various members of the band, showed them how the food was prepared, and how the Merrie Men spent their time.

Marian said that she, like Robin, could be happy in the forest. She soon settled down to her new life, and quickly endeared herself to the outlaw company. Robin and she were specially happy and they decided to marry and go on living in the forest together.

The wedding took place on a spring evening. Robin and Marian stood under the fresh green leaves of a tall oak tree; above them the green-leaved branches hung gracefully down, like the tracery-roof of a cathedral. Birds sang in the boughs. Friar Tuck stood in front of the couple, and around them stood the Merrie Men in silence. Marian had made a wedding dress for herself, and she looked beautiful as she stood by the side of her lover. Robin's men had smartened up their clothes of Lincoln green for this great occasion. Little John and Will Scarlet were in the forefront of the company. After the ceremony the Merrie Men sang a hymn, and Robin kissed his bride.

Twang! An arrow whizzed through the air and embedded itself in the tree behind Robin and Marian. "Whoever winged that arrow shall die!" cried Robin, and ordering a group of his men to guard her with their lives, he ran through the greenwood and saw a strong band of the Sheriff's men, who'd been attracted by the outlaws' singing.

The Sheriff's men stood in one long line and their bright coats made them easy targets. Only twelve of Robin's men were armed, but their suits of Lincoln green gave them an advantage. Robin gave his orders and his men took up their positions, and kept up a continuous barrage of arrows, hitting so many of the Sheriff's men that he decided to retire—with an arrow through his hat!

"Shall we follow them, master?" cried Little John.

"No!" replied Robin with a smile. "Have you forgotten that this is my wedding day?"

One day, Little John thought of a new trick he'd play on the Sheriff, and without telling Robin the details he went to Sir Richard of Lea and told the knight he was tired of life in the greenwood and would like to become one of his soldiers. Sir Richard agreed, though he felt that Little John had a secret reason for wishing to join his service.

Dressed in scarlet livery, Little John, who was the finest archer in Sir Richard's service, led the good knight's men into Nottingham to try their skill at archery. The Sheriff, amazed at Little John's skill, gave him the prize and asked him to join *his* service.

"What's your name?" asked the Sheriff.

"Reynold Greenleaf," said the giant.

Sir Richard was unwilling to allow the giant to serve under the Sheriff, but, noticing a twinkle in Little John's eye, he guessed that this had been the outlaw's plan from the beginning, and he agreed to let him go.

"I'll pay you double your present wage, Reynold Greenleaf," said the Sheriff.

So Little John entered the Sheriff's service. He discovered that the Sheriff was mean to his servants, for they rarely received their wages at the proper time, and the food was poor.

One day, the Sheriff went with some of his men to a distant town, leaving the giant in charge of his castle. The steward, who'd been left to feed the remaining guards, was lazy, and didn't offer Little

John anything to eat. So, after the Sheriff had left, the giant entered the kitchen and demanded some food. But when the steward told him to get it himself, Little John knocked him out, and helped himself to a fine meal. Then the burly cook came in, and, guessing that the giant had knocked out the steward in order to steal some food, set upon Little John, who in turn set upon him.

When the fight was over, Little John, revealing his true identity, invited the cook to join the outlaws. "I'll go with you," said the cook, "but we must hurry away before the steward wakens up."

"The Sheriff owes me some wages," said Little John.

"He owes me some, too," said the cook.

"Then we'll pay ourselves and charge the Sheriff interest," laughed Little John, and gathering a bag of gold, and all the Sheriff's silver dishes—which they crammed into two sacks—they went to the outlaws' camp.

"Why are you wearing the Sheriff's colours, Little John?" asked Robin.

"I'm one of the Sheriff's men, or rather, I *was*!"

Robin laughed heartily when he heard the whole story.

Early next day, Little John persuaded Robin to have the Sheriff's dishes set out on the table, ready for a meal, and to have the Sheriff's cook there to wait on him, then, dressed in the clothes the Sheriff had given him when he'd entered his service, he ran through the forest to the Nottingham road, for he was sure the Sheriff would return that day, and he wanted to catch him before he arrived at his castle. When presently the Sheriff appeared, riding ahead of his men, Little John, stopping him, said he'd seen a very large hart, and—knowing the Sheriff was a keen hunter—offered to take him to the spot.

Ordering his men to return to Nottingham, the Sheriff said, "Lead the way, Reynold Greenleaf!"

The outlaw led him straight to Robin's camp, and the Sheriff knew he was trapped, and when he sat down and saw his own cook serving a meal on his own dishes he groaned.

Robin made the Sheriff dress in Lincoln green and stay the night. Next morning, Robin said to the Sheriff, "You are in our power, and we could easily kill you, but we'll spare you if you'll swear friendship to us for ever."

"It's more than I'd have done for you," said the Sheriff, "but I'll be your

friend and I shall seek your life no more."

So Robin sent away the Sheriff, who kept his promise loyally; but as often as he missed his fine silver he wondered how he could free himself of his promise to Robin.

When the Sheriff's wife heard that her husband had promised not to hunt the outlaws she was furious. But he said he couldn't go back on his word. "If you want to get round your promise," she said, craftily, "just announce a shooting match in Nottingham, and if the prize is good enough Robin Hood will be there, and when he wins the contest—as he's sure to do—let him see that you recognize him when he comes for his prize. Secretly order your men to attack him, and you, yourself, allow him to escape before they reach him. You'll then be quits."

"It's a cunning plan," admitted the Sheriff, "and after that I can seek to capture the outlaw and bring him to justice."

News of the contest spread quickly, and when Robin learned that the prize was to be a silver arrow he decided to enter. "The silver arrow will be a fine present for Marian," he said.

His men tried to dissuade him from going to Nottingham in case he should be captured. "The Sheriff won't go back on his word," said Robin, "but to be on the safe side we'll all enter the contest."

On the day of the match, Robin and his men, all in disguise, and each carrying a bow and some arrows, went into Nottingham and mingled with the eight hundred archers who were going to shoot.

The contest was held in a meadow, at one end of which a willow-wand stood in the ground. This was to be the target. Robin decided that only the best of his men would enter the competition, the remainder standing by in case of need.

It took a long time for all the contestants to shoot, but gradually the failures dropped out, leaving only five—all of whom were Robin's men—in the match. As they took their final shots, four of them fell out, and then, amid cheers, Robin was declared the winner.

As the Sheriff presented the silver arrow to this unknown marksman, he suddenly recognized the outlaw. Turning to one of his men, he whispered the secret signal that would set the soldiers against Robin.

"It's Robin Hood, the outlaw!" cried one of the Sheriff's men.

The Sheriff whispered in Robin's ear. "Go, whilst you may! I've kept my promise, but this makes us quits!"

Robin saw through the plan, and bringing out his horn from amongst his clothes he blew it. Immediately, the meadow swarmed with the outlaws, and after a great battle, in which the Sheriff's men were driven back, Robin ordered his men back to the forest. But on the way an arrow from one of the Sheriff's men embedded itself in Little John's knee, and he fell. "Don't wait for me, master," he said. "Stab me so I shan't die by the rope, then leave me."

Robin, taking no notice of his faithful friend's pleas, called Much-the-Miller's son, and together they lifted Little John and staggered on with him.

"We've only one chance," said Robin, as the Sheriff's men were hot on their heels. "We must make for Sir Richard of Lea's castle. We could never get back to the forest before the Sheriff's men catch up with us."

Stumbling bravely across fields, they arrived at Sir Richard's castle with their burden just before the Sheriff's men.

Sir Richard welcomed them, and soon the three outlaws were resting in his castle. The Sheriff's men, aware that it would be impossible to force their way into the stone fortress, gave up the chase and returned to Nottingham.

Robin showed his silver arrow prize to Sir Richard, who said, "Maid Marian will be very proud of this—and of you."

When at last Robin returned to the forest, he presented the prize to his wife, who treasured it always, and seldom allowed it out of her sight.

Robin Hood was a master of disguise, and in a secret forest lodge he had all sorts of disguises, which he used from time to time. One day, how-

ever, to the dismay of Little John, Will Scarlet, Much-the-Miller's son, and the other outlaws, he announced his intention of going to church in Nottingham without any disguise, and refused to allow anybody to escort him. Little John thought such boldness was asking for trouble and tried to dissuade him. But Robin's mind was made up, and off he went.

It so happened that a monk whom Robin had relieved of moneybags in the forest attended church that morning. The monk, recognizing Robin, sent word to the Sheriff, who knew that if he took no action questions would be asked about his loyalty to the King. He could do nothing but send armed men to capture Robin in the church. Besides, was he not now free to seek the outlaw's capture again?

Half-way through the service the Sheriff's men advanced down the aisle towards him. "You varlets!" he cried. "Cannot a man go to church in peace?"

Though he fought desperately, Robin was overpowered and dragged away to a dungeon where he was chained hand and foot. How he wished he'd taken Little John's advice!

The Sheriff realized that the King would have to be informed about Robin's capture, and that meant he'd be kept in captivity until the Sheriff's messenger returned with the King's orders.

It was the monk himself who offered to go to Westminster with the news, and that same day he set off alone on the journey to London.

Back in the greenwood camp, the outlaws were worried when Robin didn't return from church. So Little John and Much-the-Miller's son decided to go to Nottingham to find out what had happened. At a friend's cottage on the Nottingham road they learned of Robin's capture. Presently, they met a mounted monk coming along the road from Nottingham. "Ho, Sir Monk!" cried Little John. "Is there any more news of the capture of Robin Hood?"

"Well," said the monk, stopping his horse, "the outlaw is captured at last and will meet justice. It was I who first recognized him in church, and it's I who am taking the news to the King of England for his instructions."

"Bravo!" cried Little John. "But what would you do if you were to meet Robin Hood's band along the road?"

"Have no fear," said the monk. "None of his band would know my mission."

Little John gave a knowing wink to Much-the-Miller's son, then the two outlaws offered to accompany the monk for part of the way, and the monk accepted their offer gratefully, for he was rather fearful of meeting Robin's band. The three men travelled about a mile to a spot where the road became very lonely and deserted, and Much-the-Miller's son whispered to Little John that the time had come to end the monk's journey to London. They rode on for a short distance farther, then they suddenly attacked. The monk had no time to wonder what it all meant, for Little John jumped upon his back, dragged him off his horse, pulled the cowl down over his face, and tied him up securely. Then

they escorted him, blindfolded, through the secret paths of Sherwood Forest to their camp, where they left him in charge of faithful followers of Robin Hood.

One evening, a week after Robin had been captured, Little John and Much-the-Miller's son, disguised as travellers, arrived at the Sheriff's castle with a letter supposed to be from the King of England. The Sheriff took them into his dining-room, but Little John kept in the shadows so that the Sheriff wouldn't recognize him, for he knew him as Reynold Greenleaf. So it was Much-the-Miller's son who handed the Sheriff the letter.

"Where's the monk who took the message to London?" asked the Sheriff.

"The King has kept him there," replied Much-the-Miller's son.

The Sheriff read the letter, which ordered that Robin should be taken to London, then he invited his guests to dine with him while they discussed the best way of getting their prisoner to London. As soon as the servants had left the room, however, Little John clapped his hand over the Sheriff's mouth, so that he couldn't cry out, while Much-the-Miller's son tied him to his chair. Then the two outlaws left the castle and ran through the streets. Such a strong guard had been placed around the gates of Nottingham that none of Robin's band had yet been able to get inside the city to free their leader, but Little John and Much-the-Miller's son now had a chance of rescue, for somewhere in the side of the fortress rock there was a cave, at the end of which lay the dungeon where Robin was kept prisoner.

It was Much-the-Miller's son who stumbled across the cave entrance,

which was partly covered by bushes. Hearing the sound of his stumbling, a sentry ran to the cave-mouth, but Little John felled him with a single blow.

The two men ran into the cave, stopping when they came to a locked door. "Stand clear!" said Little John, charging the door, which gave way under his great weight. In front of them was a flight of stone steps, at the top of which stood a sentry. "Ho, sentry!" called Little John, from the darkness at the bottom of the steps.

Grasping a torch, the sentry came down the steps and Little John felled him like a log. Other voices could now be heard, for Little John had made more noise than was safe. "Robin Hood's escaped!" he shouted.

"Which way did he go?" said another sentry, who couldn't see Little John in the shadows. The giant said that he'd run down the stairs and out through the cave. The sentry ran on, followed by a second guard. But a third knocked on a cell door.

"What's ado?" cried the voice of Robin Hood from within.

"Whoever has escaped, it isn't Robin Hood," cried the sentry.

"Not yet," said Little John, striking the sentry a blow that sent him reeling to the ground, and picking up the keys dropped by one of the warders, and finding one that fitted the lock, he thrust open the heavy cell door, and soon Much-the-Miller's son freed Robin from his chains.

"Bravely done!" said Robin, standing up and stretching his cramped body.

Suddenly, four men with swords rushed into the dark cell. Robin dragged his companions out of the door, then slammed it shut, locking the four soldiers in the cell.

"I shall go out the way I came in," said Robin. "By the main entrance."

It was a daring plan, but marching out boldly, with a score of other men who were ordered to raise the alarm, Robin and his friends made good their escape, and all who met the three outlaws took them to be some of the soldiers that had come from Wakefield and Pontefract to make the garrison larger.

Robin Hood was a free man again.

One day, Robin was walking along the Nottingham road when he met two men. "Good afternoon," he said, pleasantly. But the men were rude to Robin, and one threatened to knock his head off. "You are welcome to try," said Robin, who wasn't afraid of them.

"We are messengers from the Bishop of Hereford," said the other man. "We are on our way to Nottingham to deliver a message to the Sheriff. We do not intend to be hindered by such as you."

"But you are hindered," replied Robin, "and, what's more, you're going to spend the night with me."

The two men laughed, but a moment later Little John came up, and when Robin told him the two men were to spend the night with them, the outlaws soon overpowered the men and escorted them back to the camp, where they spent the night.

The next morning Robin called Will Scarlet and Will Gamwell, and said he had a dangerous job for them if they would do it. When they said they would, Robin said, "I've read the letter those two messengers were taking to the Sheriff of Nottingham. In it the Bishop of Hereford asks for a loan of two hundred pounds. He says it's urgent and very important. I want you to impersonate the two messengers and go to the Sheriff with this letter. It'll be fun to disappoint the Bishop and at the same time score against the Sheriff.

The two Wills, dressed in the messengers' clothes, took the letter, and set out for the Sheriff's castle. When they arrived they handed the letter to the Sheriff, who read it in silence. "Two hundred pounds is a lot of money," he said. "I don't think I have that much money with me."

"Then we'd better take what you have," said Will Scarlet. "The Bishop will be very angry if we go back with nothing."

So the Sheriff gave the men a hundred and fifty pounds—all he could find. The two Wills thanked the Sheriff and walked out. But at the castle gate they came face to face with the Bishop of Hereford, who'd decided, after his messengers had set out, that a personal visit would be more likely to secure the loan.

The two Wills took to their heels, but they hadn't gone far before the Sheriff learned from the Bishop that they were impostors. Immediately, the Sheriff and his men gave chase.

Not having time to return safely to the forest, the two Wills ran to Sir Richard of Lea's castle. The good knight welcomed them, and, guessing that the Sheriff would attack the main gate, he ordered the planks of the drawbridge to be loosened so that they were just resting on their cross-supports.

A few minutes later the Sheriff's men, headed by the Sheriff and the Bishop, charged across the drawbridge, which had been left down. Then, as Sir Richard's men raised the drawbridge, the loosened boards slipped off into the moat, and the men (except the Sheriff and the Bishop, who'd reached the end of the drawbridge) fell with them!

The two Wills carried a bucket of paste to a room above the drawbridge and poured it through holes in the floor on to the heads of the Bishop and Sheriff, who were hanging like monkeys on to the gate! The sticky paste covered the Bishop and the Sheriff, and, loosening their grip, they fell with a splash into the moat!

All thoughts of money forgotten for the moment, the Sheriff and the Bishop swam the moat and returned with the other wet men to the Sheriff's castle!

The two Wills dined with Sir Richard, and after thanking him for his kindness in helping them to escape they made their way back to Robin Hood and his Merrie Men.

The Sheriff was still dripping with paste when he reached home, and he immediately doubled the price on Robin Hood's head. An armed band, eager to get the reward, set out for the

forest. Robin and Marian had gone away visiting, the day of the attack, and they wouldn't be back until nightfall.

"There's trouble ahead," exclaimed Will Scarlet. "Armed men are coming towards us."

The outlaws took up their positions to face the attack, but so many of them were out on hunting expeditions that there weren't enough to defend the camp properly. The band of advancing men knew they'd be no match for the outlaws if they fought man to man. Their only chance was to wound some of them from a distance, and that's just what they did, wounding Will the Wrestler and his two brothers, Lester, and Harry, who fell to the ground.

This was enough for the band of men, who captured the outlaws and returned to Nottingham with them.

The Sheriff was delighted. "They'll be hanged tomorrow!" he announced.

When Robin came home to the forest and heard from a poor widow—the mother of Will the Wrestler and his two brothers—that her sons had been captured, he promised to do all he could to rescue them.

Early next morning, as Robin was on his way to Nottingham, he met an old palmer, who said he was going to town to pray for the three condemned men. Robin had a sudden inspiration. He begged the palmer to exchange some clothes with him so that he could attend the hanging instead, but the palmer refused. However, the jingling of money soon changed his mind, and shortly afterwards Robin, wearing the palmer's robes, walked through the city gate of Nottingham and went straight to the scaffold, where the three brothers were standing bound and ready for the hanging.

"Good Sheriff," cried the palmer, "it's surely right that these three varlets should have a chance to repent before they die."

"They'll have plenty of time for that," said the Sheriff. "I can get nobody to hang them."

"Let me do it," pleaded the palmer. "Justice must be done."

The Sheriff was relieved when he heard this, but the crowd jeered as the palmer stepped on the platform. "It's your leader," whispered Robin to the condemned men. "Have no fear, I'll set you free, and then, when I give the word, we must fight our way out of here." Swiftly, Robin loosened their bonds, but the men stood still, pretending that they were still tied. Luckily, the Sheriff was unaware of what had happened.

Suddenly, Robin threw off the palmer's robes and stood revealed in Lincoln green. Putting his horn to his lips, he blew three sharp blasts, and in a few moments the outlaws raced towards the execution-place. "Run for it, and fight for your lives!" cried Robin to the three brothers.

The three men, with Robin at their head, battled their way out of the crowd with their fists. The Sheriff's men gathered quickly together and awaited orders, but they had lost too much time, for Robin and the three brothers were running towards their friends in Lincoln green, who were now near the scene.

Desperately, the Sheriff lined up his men. "Your weapons," he cried. "Where are your weapons?"

"We laid them in a heap on the ground just before the execution was due to take place," said one of his men.

"Then get them, varlets, get them!" stormed the Sheriff.

The men broke ranks and ran to retrieve their spears and swords, then they began to line up again.

Escape was complete by the time the Sheriff and his men were properly mustered. Robin's men far outnumbered the few soldiers that had gathered to watch the executions, and the Sheriff could do nothing but look on hopelessly at the distant figures who were vanishing quickly in the direction of Sherwood Forest.

After Widow Hardlock (for that was her name) had expressed her gratitude to Robin for rescuing her three sons, he went hunting alone in the forest.

Suddenly, he met the Bishop of Hereford, who said he'd a debt to pay him.

"I'm always ready to accept a debt," laughed Robin.

"This is no laughing matter," said the Bishop. "You robbed me of money loaned to me by the Sheriff of Nottingham, and now I'll rob you of your laugh."

"If that's your mood," sighed Robin, "we'll go our own ways."

As Robin walked away, the Bishop gave chase on his horse, so Robin ran among the trees where the horse couldn't easily follow, and when he came to Widow Hardlock's cottage, he said, "Good dame, I must hide at once, for the Bishop of Hereford's after me."

When the Bishop came to the cottage he dismounted and knocked on the door. "Come in," called a voice.

"Have you seen an outlaw in Lincoln green?" said the Bishop, eyeing the widow, who was working at her loom.

"No," she answered, "but look for yourself."

Suddenly, the Bishop heard a movement in a cupboard. He opened the door, and there, huddled in a corner, was Robin Hood.

The trapped man walked out of the cupboard and was led away by the Bishop, leaving the widow at her loom.

Back in the forest, Little John and Will Scarlet saw what they thought was Widow Hardlock. But it wasn't the widow; it was Robin, who, after taking refuge in her cottage, had changed clothes with her. "If the Bishop had known it was Robin Hood sitting at the loom, he'd have been furious!" laughed Robin.

Having summoned his men with three blasts on his horn, Robin changed clothes with one of them, then he and his band set out and soon caught up with the Bishop, who looked in bewilderment from Robin to the widow in Lincoln green!

At Robin's suggestion, Widow Hardlock boxed the Bishop's ears for taking her away by force, and Robin ordered the Bishop to pay her the exact sum of money she'd have made had she been working all the time. Then, allowing the Bishop to leave, he escorted the widow to their camp, where she was to be the guest of honour at a feast.

About a week later the Bishop of Hereford with fifty
armed men set out to find Robin's camp and capture
him, but not knowing exactly where it was he asked Little John and
Will Scarlet, who were out in search of adventure disguised as
tramps. Misdirecting the Bishop, the two outlaws ran to tell Robin,
who, with a number of his band, went after the Bishop, who was
not far from a muddy swamp. When the Bishop saw the outlaws he
gave chase, and Robin and his men lured him straight into
the swamp, while avoiding it themselves. When the Bishop's
men saw him floundering in the mud, having been thrown
off his horse, they fled, for Robin's men had
them covered with their arrows.

"Save me, Robin Hood!" pleaded the
Bishop, "and I'll cause you no
more trouble!"

The outlaws rescued the Bishop, took him to their camp, gave him a suit of Lincoln green to wear (for his own clothes were ruined), and, after a hearty meal of the King's venison, escorted him out of the forest.

Walking one day in the forest, Robin and Marian met a young man called Alan-a-Dale, who was miserable because Ellen, the girl he loved, was being forced against her will to marry a Norman baron. Robin said he'd stop the wedding if Alan and Ellen would join the outlaws, and Alan agreed.

The next day, Robin and his men went to the Abbey where the wedding was about to take place and Robin declared to the Bishop, "Ellen will marry the man she loves."

"Alan-a-Dale's the man I love," cried Ellen.

Pushing the Bishop aside, Friar Tuck promptly married the happy couple, who returned with Robin to the greenwood.

One day in the following spring, Alan-a-Dale, Ellen, and Friar Tuck, who were hiding behind a tree, saw a mendicant friar relieve two black monks of their moneybags, after they'd deceived him by pretending they had no money. Needless to say, the mendicant friar was Robin Hood!

Robin, Will Scarlet, and Little John were crossing a field one day when they came to a stile. Robin started to clamber over it when he was stopped by a

gruff voice on the other side. "Where d'you think you're going? Don't you know the difference between a field and a road?"

It was the voice of the Pinder, who was not only responsible for rounding up stray cattle which were herded inside pounds until their owners paid a fine for letting them stray, but also, as Highway Officer, for stopping people from walking across fields when they should keep to the roads. With a stout staff in his hand, the Pinder waited for stray cattle and people. He made sure everyone paid the correct fine, whether the owner was a lord or a peasant; he thus became known as the honest Pinder.

Robin said, "Do you know who I am?"

"I neither know nor care," answered the Pinder. "I just make people pay if they stray on to these fields."

"How do you make them pay if they're three to one, as we are?" asked Robin.

"I don't care if they're thirty to one—I can crack the head of any man," said the Pinder.

Robin, drawing his sword, rushed at the Pinder, but the Pinder knocked the sword out of his hand and it fell to the ground, and when Will Scarlet and Little John attempted to cross, they were repulsed in the same way.

Robin admired the man's pluck, and asked him what the trespass fee was. On being told, he paid him twice as much. "I am Robin Hood," said Robin. "Why not be one of my Merrie Men and live in the greenwood with me?"

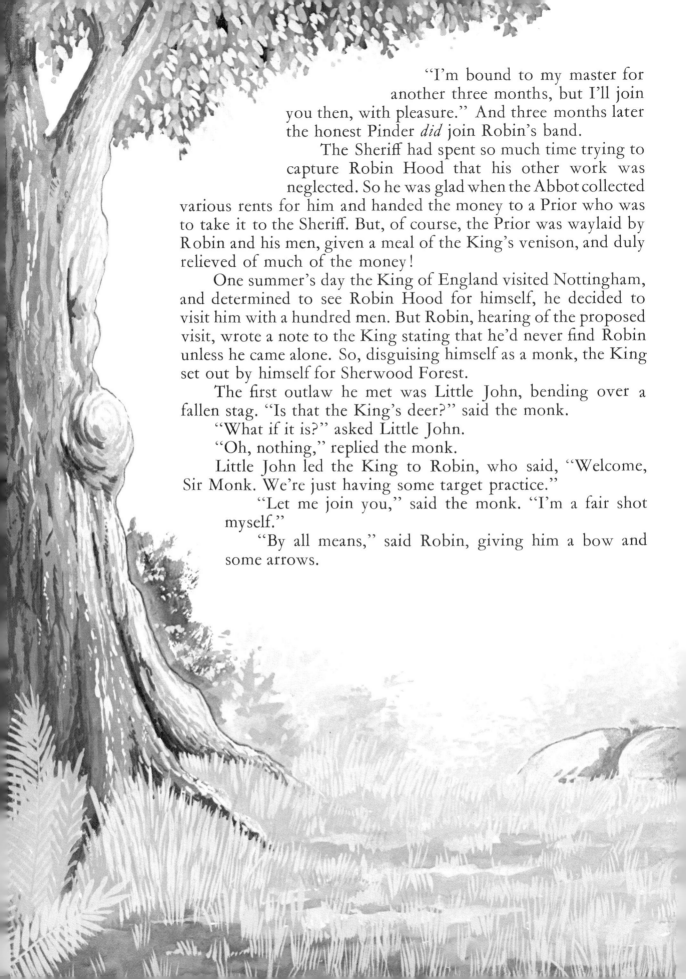

"I'm bound to my master for another three months, but I'll join you then, with pleasure." And three months later the honest Pinder *did* join Robin's band.

The Sheriff had spent so much time trying to capture Robin Hood that his other work was neglected. So he was glad when the Abbot collected various rents for him and handed the money to a Prior who was to take it to the Sheriff. But, of course, the Prior was waylaid by Robin and his men, given a meal of the King's venison, and duly relieved of much of the money!

One summer's day the King of England visited Nottingham, and determined to see Robin Hood for himself, he decided to visit him with a hundred men. But Robin, hearing of the proposed visit, wrote a note to the King stating that he'd never find Robin unless he came alone. So, disguising himself as a monk, the King set out by himself for Sherwood Forest.

The first outlaw he met was Little John, bending over a fallen stag. "Is that the King's deer?" said the monk.

"What if it is?" asked Little John.

"Oh, nothing," replied the monk.

Little John led the King to Robin, who said, "Welcome, Sir Monk. We're just having some target practice."

"Let me join you," said the monk. "I'm a fair shot myself."

"By all means," said Robin, giving him a bow and some arrows.

Robin, introducing the monk to Sir Richard of Lea, said, "Sir Richard isn't one of my band, but he's here to-day because we're expecting a visit from the King, and he's one of the King's most loyal servants."

"Then you must be Robin Hood," said the monk.

Robin bowed and suggested that any who couldn't hit the target receive a punch from his neighbour.

The marksmen lined up, and when it was the monk's turn his arrow hit the bull's-eye. But Robin's aim was slightly off, and since he was next to the monk he received a hard knock from him.

"You have a strong arm, good monk," said Robin. "Take off your cowl and let us see you clearly."

The monk refused, and Robin knocked him to the ground. Up he sprang, however, and knocked Robin to the ground. "You're a man after my own heart," laughed Robin. "You should join my Merrie Men."

Sir Richard came to help Robin up, then, turning to the monk, he sank down upon one knee before him. "Your Majesty!" said Sir Richard.

The outlaws, realizing that they were standing before the King, followed Sir Richard's example.

"Stand, men!" ordered the King. "I've seen what brave men you are, and I'll offer you

all a free pardon if you'll join my service.

Robin, thinking it would be better for Marian if he joined the King's service, accepted the offer. A few days later, when the King set out for London, he was accompanied by Robin, Marian, and many of the Merrie Men. But the King allowed some of the outlaws to return to their homes and start a trade.

But life at court didn't suit Robin, and the King gave him a fortnight's leave to visit Sherwood Forest again. Robin left London immediately, and Marian followed later in a horse-drawn wagon. Meanwhile, the other outlaws who'd gone with Robin to London had gradually left the King's service and returned to the forest. Determined that Robin shouldn't go back to London, Little John and Will Scarlet pounced on him, and he was held captive while Will Scarlet went to see the King. On his return, Will said to Robin, "I told the King you were held captive against your will; that the forest was your true home and that you'd never be happy at court. The King said that you and all the Merrie Men can stay in Sherwood Forest on condition that you'd be at his service, if ever the country is in danger. I gave him that assurance, master."

Robin was overjoyed at the news, and all the outlaws in the forest were summoned to the camp for a feast to celebrate his return to the old life of freedom and adventure.

During Robin's absence from the greenwood a new Sheriff had been elected at Nottingham. He was a weak man, who rarely interfered with anything that happened, whether right or wrong. However, the Sheriff's finest swordsman determined to capture Robin Hood, and, persuading the Sheriff to go to the forest with him, he captured Little John, had him bound to a tree, and went deeper into the forest, while the Sheriff guarded the giant.

The swordsman, covering his armour with a horse-skin, which made him look like a vagabond, followed two of Robin's men who were carrying a deer, and he was sure they hadn't seen him. But they *had*! So leading him to the camp, they warned Robin that a man was following. Robin blew his horn, and the swordsman was soon surrounded by outlaws.

"Robin Hood," said the swordsman, "I've sworn to the Sheriff of Nottingham to take you back with me. Little John is bound to a tree." Then he challenged Robin to a fight.

"Choose your weapons," said Robin.

The Sheriff's man was a brilliant swordsman, so of course, he chose the sword.

The combat began. Robin fought with great skill. His thrusts and parries were quicker than those of his foe, but his opponent fought ruthlessly and fiercely. At length, however, he started to tire, for he was older than Robin. The outlaw pressed him harder than

ever. Slowly, he wore him down, then, with a savage thrust, Robin struck him in an unguarded moment, and the swordsman fell with a groan, never to rise again.

The cheers that greeted Robin's victory echoed through the forest. Robin ordered the swordsman's clothes to be taken from him, and the corpse buried. This done, Robin, wearing the slain man's attire, set out to free Little John.

He found the giant, still tied to a tree, with the Sheriff of Nottingham standing guard over him. The Sheriff looked relieved when he saw Robin, believing him to be his swordsman.

"Ho, there, Sheriff!" called Robin. "Robin Hood is slain. Allow me to loosen the bonds of this varlet so that we can take him for public hanging in Nottingham." So saying, he untied Little John, whispering to the giant as he did so who he was.

When he'd freed Little John, Robin threw off the swordsman's clothing, revealing his suit of Lincoln green.

The Sheriff was too terrified to move. He stood aghast, staring at the two outlaws.

"Ha, ha, Little John!" laughed Robin. "What do you think of a Sheriff of Nottingham who cannot move himself backwards or forwards?"

Robin strode up to the Sheriff and said, "Go, good Sheriff, for I have no wish to harm you; only never venture into the forest alone, lest Robin Hood bite you!"

The Sheriff needed no urging. He turned and ran to where his horse was standing, and in a matter of seconds he was galloping towards Nottingham.

Laughing heartily, Robin Hood and Little John linked arms and strolled off to their camp deep in the heart of the greenwood.

Clement of the Glen, a married man who hadn't seen his wife for a long time, was one of Robin's outlaws. There'd been trouble in the village where he lived, and his only chance of escape had been to join Robin and his band. "If I could see my wife again I should feel at peace," he said to Robin, who advised him to do so as soon as he could.

So he set off, and his wife was happy indeed when she saw him and took him into the cottage. "I've taken in a lodger," she said. "She's an old lady who pays generously and I'm able to live on the money she gives me."

Clement noticed the old lady sitting in the darkened kitchen; but his thoughts were only for his wife. But the old lady, who knew the circumstances that had sent Clement away, was offended because he hadn't greeted her, and, full of resentment, she went and told one of the Sheriff's men that he was back. She didn't return to the cottage, however, for she knew that action would soon follow.

When Clement saw the Sheriff's men coming, he and his wife placed furniture against the bolted door, then Clement armed himself with a bow-and-arrow, while his wife brandished a chopper.

Realizing that they couldn't enter the cottage without injury to themselves, the leader of the Sheriff's men cried "Burn the place down!"

As the flames engulfed the front of the cottage, Clement raced to the back, helped his wife out of the window, and told her to run into the forest, where he'd join her later. Then, returning to the front, he put up a brave fight, but was overpowered and cast into prison.

Meanwhile, a lad from the town ran to tell Robin Hood that Clement had been captured and was going to be hanged. There was no time to lose, so Robin and Little John hurried to the prison, demanded to be let in, and when the porter opened the door Robin crashed his fist on the man's jaw, snatched his keys, and rushed to Clement's cell, followed by Little John. They soon had the cell open, and were about to leave when they saw the Sheriff approaching. The three outlaws stopped in their tracks.

"You're trapped in my own prison," said the Sheriff, leaning against the recently-erected scaffold.

Suddenly, Robin shot an arrow which pierced the Sheriff's coat, pinning him to the scaffold.

"Help!" bellowed the Sheriff. But the three outlaws sped on and were almost out of Nottingham before the chase had been organized.

Bursting into the forest, they came upon a woman who was weeping. "That's my wife," cried Clement of the Glen in delight.

That day, another member was added to Robin Hood's band, for Clement's

wife joined them in the forest and made her home there. She was welcomed by Maid Marian, and she soon learned to love the friendly ways of the greenwood.

Robin lived in the greenwood for many more years, but as they grew older many of the outlaws died and were buried in the forest.

When Marian became old, Robin sent her to live in Kirke Hall Priory, where he thought she'd be more comfortable than in the forest. Little John was now grey-haired, and one spring morning Robin said to him, "I'm old, and before I die I want to see Marian once more."

So the two aged outlaws set off for the nunnery. But when they arrived the Prioress told Robin that Marian had died.

Grief-stricken, Robin went upstairs to the room where Marian had spent her last days. Little John remained below with Robin's bow. Feeling weak, Robin blew three faint blasts on his horn, and Little John rushed upstairs with his master's bow.

Robin took the bow and, going to the window, fired his last arrow. It landed far in the forest that had been his home. "I'm dying, Little John," he said, feebly, "and when I'm gone bury me where my arrow has fallen."

Little John buried Robin Hood as he'd wished, but the memory of his adventures will live on for ever.